PETER PAN AND WENDY

Also available as paperback classics
from Macmillan Children's Books

Alice's Adventures in Wonderland
The Jungle Book
The Second Jungle Book
Just So Stories
Kim
Puck of Pook's Hill
Rewards and Fairies
The Water-Babies

MABEL
LUCIE
ATTWELL

PETER PAN AND WENDY

J. M. BARRIE

Illustrated by Mabel Lucie-Attwell

MACMILLAN
CHILDREN'S BOOKS

J. M. Barrie's *Peter and Wendy* was first published by Hodder & Stoughton Ltd in 1911.
May Byron's retelling for children containing original illustrations by Mabel Lucie Attwell was
first published as J.M. Barrie's *Peter Pan and Wendy* in 1921 by Hodder and Stoughton Ltd.
Further May Byron abridgements were also published for 'little people' and
'boys and girls', all containing the original Mabel Lucie Attwell artwork.

This edition published 2018 by Macmillan Children's Books
an imprint of Pan Macmillan
20 New Wharf Road, London N1 9RR
Associated companies throughout the world
www.panmacmillan.com

ISBN 978-1-5098-6995-4
Retold by May Byron for little people with the approval of the author

Illustrations copyright © Lucie Attwell Ltd
The right of Mabel Lucie Attwell to be identified as the illustrator of this work has been asserted
by BWA Design LLP in accordance with the Copyright, Designs and Patents Act 1988.

This edition of J. M. Barrie's *Peter Pan and Wendy* published by arrangement with
Great Ormond Street Hospital Children's Charity.

Pan Macmillan does not have any control over, or any responsibility for,
any author or third-party websites referred to in or on this book.

1 3 5 7 9 8 6 4 2

A CIP catalogue record for this book is available from the British Library.

Typeset by The Dimpse
Printed and bound by CPI Group (UK) Ltd, Croydon CR0 4YY

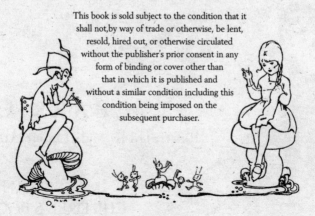

Contents

1

The Family at No.14

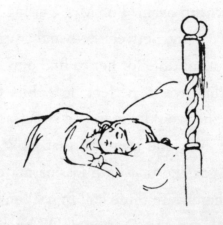

All children, except one, grow up. They soon know that they will grow up, and the way Wendy Moira Angela Darling knew was this: one day when she was two years old she was playing in a garden, and she ran to her mother with some flowers she had picked. And she looked so sweet, just like a little flower herself, that Mrs Darling said, "Oh, why can't you stay like this for ever!"

Then Wendy began to see that one didn't stay at two for the rest of one's life. Indeed, two is the beginning of the end. The end is being grown-up. Once you get to twenty-one or so, you can never be un-grown-up again. But Mrs Darling did not tell this to Wendy. Between two and twenty-one, there was lots of time for her to find out.

Mrs Darling was a perfect dear. Just the sort of mother one would choose: as sweet as honey, with lovely eyes, and a mouth that looked like a kiss. It had got like that with kissing her children so often. There were three children: Wendy, John and Michael; and Mrs Darling didn't know which she loved best. They were all pretty good, but Wendy was the best, because she tried to make herself as like her mother as could be. It wasn't easy of course, but still she tried.

The three little Darlings had a very nice nursery, with lots of toys and picture-books; also a night-nursery with three little beds in it. And they had a most uncommon kind of nurse. She was called Nana, like other nurses, but she was

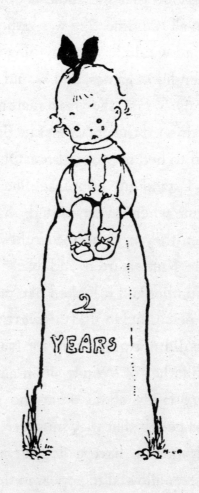

really a large Newfoundland dog. Her kennel was in the nursery, so that she could keep her eye on the children all the time. She was rather prim and particular, and would have everything just so, but she was splendid at games, and would join in the wildest romps. In fact, she was a real treasure: she bathed and dressed the children, saw that they got up and went to bed in proper time. Oh, I tell you, she wouldn't stand any nonsense! She gave them their medicine when it was wanted, changed their pinnies when they became too grubby, and took them to the Kindergarten and back every day, carrying an umbrella if it looked like rain.

The only person at No. 14 (this was the Darlings' house) who did not much care for Nana was Mr Darling, the father of Wendy, John and Michael. He was very faddy about what the neighbours thought, and he felt that they must certainly think it extremely odd to have a dog for a nurse. So Nana was never allowed to appear in the drawing-room, and if visitors came, she was shut up in the nursery, while the door was opened by the tiny little maidservant, Liza. Everybody knew that Mr Darling was not the best of friends with Nana, but everybody pretended not to know. It was a pity he was so set against her.

However, the children had other things to take up their minds. When the Kindergarten part of the day was over and it wasn't time yet for the evening romps and dances, they talked to each other about the Never-Land. One could go on doing that for hours.

The Never-Land was a make-believe island, full of delightful places and interesting people. It is very hard to describe, because an island of that sort changes about from day to day, according to how you want it to be. It might be all over fairies, dwarfs and goblins; or it might have giants who live in enchanted castles, and princes (always the youngest of three) who go and attack them. Or it might have a robbers' cave, and a tumble-down cottage where a witch makes magic. There could be pirates there, too, and all sorts of ships (that's where an island comes in so useful), and coral reefs, and underground rivers. There is no end to the wonderful things in the Never-Land.

The most wonderful of all, though, is Peter Pan.

Now, Mrs Darling knew, more or less, about the Never-Land. Very likely, when she was little, she had had a make-believe island of her own, cram-full of flowers, and kisses, and fairy ladies. As time went on, she forgot about it; still, she liked to hear what the children had to tell her. There was one thing, however, which puzzled her: and that was the name Peter Pan. Wendy had the most to say about him; but John and Michael mentioned him now and then. When Mrs Darling asked, "But who is Peter Pan?" nobody could explain; only Wendy said that he wasn't a grown-up person, he was just her size. Wendy was now about nine. Mrs Darling thought perhaps he was some boy at the Kindergarten.

But one day, Wendy told her that Peter sometimes came in the night, and sat at the end of her bed, playing on his pipes. No Kindergarten boy would do that. Besides, he couldn't get into

the house without somebody knowing.

So Mrs Darling said that Wendy was talking nonsense. Nobody could come in at night like that.

Wendy replied that it was not nonsense; Peter came in by the window. She said, "You know those funny leaves that were on the floor today by the window? You couldn't think what they were?"

Mrs Darling certainly had picked up some strange unknown leaves. She said: "What have leaves got to do with Peter Pan?"

They are off his shoes," said Wendy. "Naughty boy, he will not wipe his shoes. He never does."

"Why have you never told me all this before?" asked her mother.

"I suppose I forgot," said Wendy.

Mrs Darling was very uneasy, and she searched all over the nursery to see if the naughty boy was hiding anywhere. She asked Mr Darling if he had ever heard of a person called Peter Pan. But he said, "Oh dear me! It's some silly stuff that Nana has been putting into the children's heads. What do you expect if you will have a dog for a nurse?" She thought she would show him the leaves, but on second thoughts she did not.

The following evening Mrs Darling was sitting sewing by the night-nursery fire. Nana had gone out, so she herself had bathed the little ones and put them to bed. They had dropped off to sleep while she sang to them. She had lit their three night-lights, and everything was as quiet as could be. Presently, it was so peaceful that she went to sleep too.

And suddenly, the night-nursery window flew open by itself, and a lovely boy dropped in. He was dressed in leaves of every colour. When he saw a grown-up sitting there, he was very much annoyed. Mrs Darling, waking with a start, knew at once – though I can't say how she knew – that this must be Peter Pan.

2

How Mr Darling Disliked Nana

Mrs Darling cried out in her surprise, and that moment the door opened, and Nana came in. When she saw the boy, she growled and sprang at him. She did not catch him, for he leaped through the window before she could pull it down. But she caught his shadow, and brought it in her mouth to Mrs Darling. It was quite a common sort of shadow; it might have belonged to any boy.

Mrs Darling rolled it up carefully and put it away in a drawer. She was more puzzled than ever. But she knew if she told Mr Darling what she had seen, he would say it all came of having a dog for a nurse. And really Nana had done her best.

Nothing more happened until about a week later. It was Friday evening: Mr and Mrs Darling were dressing to go to a party, and Nana was busy putting the children to bed. She began, as usual, with Michael. She had put on his bath water, taken the towel in her mouth, and set Michael on her back to carry him; but Michael was cross because he couldn't stay up any longer. He shouted, and kicked, and said he wasn't going to bed. "I won't, I won't!" he cried. "And I don't love you any more, Nana!"

Mrs Darling looked so pretty that Michael became good at once. She was all in white, with a necklace that Mr Darling had given her, and a bracelet that Wendy had lent her. Wendy thought it was lovely to have a bracelet good enough to lend such a pretty lady. Mrs Darling was like a smile and a kiss and a flower all made into one.

Wendy and John were playing at being Father

and Mother. They had just had a make-believe baby born, and were ever so pleased. Michael couldn't play, because he was in his bath. It was terribly lonely being soaped and sponged – oh you can't think how particular Nana was! – just when the others were so jolly. Michael jumped out of the water, and before he was half dry he was cuddling up to Mrs Darling. Some mothers would have minded hugging a wet child, but Mrs Darling was so very sweet.

At this moment the door banged open, and slammed shut. Not by itself, of course, but because Mr Darling had rushed in, in a raving, ramping, roaring rage. Mr Darling was a kind man, but he had got what they call a short temper. That is, his temper was very good for a short while, and then very bad for a short while, and so on, turn and turn about. This was often rather awkward, because he changed so suddenly. This time the bad temper had come on all in a minute. Mr Darling had been trying to tie his party tie, and it wouldn't let him fix it. Ties are often like that, especially if they know you are in a hurry.

"What is the matter, Father dear?" said Mrs Darling.

"Matter!" yelled Mr Darling, and his eyes nearly started out of his head. "Why, this tie will tie round the bedpost all right enough, but it won't go round my neck! I've done it twenty times over, and it simply refuses to be tied!"

"Dear, dear!" said Mrs Darling. The children all tried to put on expressions showing how sorry they were, but Mr Darling took no notice. He worked himself up into an even worse rage, and went on to say that they would all be starved now. Because, he bellowed, he wouldn't go to the party unless his tie was tied properly round his neck; and if he didn't go to the party, he should never go to the office again. And then he should never earn any more money; and he and Mrs Darling and the children would become poor homeless beggars. All on account of the tie.

"Let me try, dear," said Mrs Darling, in a voice like a cooing dove. And she fastened his tie for him quite calmly and easily. The next moment Mr Darling, in wonderful good humour, was prancing about the room with Michael on his back. His short bad temper was over – until next time.

Everybody was dancing and jumping and squeaking with delight, when Nana (who generally joined in romps) hurried in. And she knocked up by accident against Mr Darling as he whirled to and fro – and a lot of her long hairs came off upon his nice new trousers. This annoyed him dreadfully, and although Mrs Darling brushed him clean, he began to talk again about how stupid it was to have a dog for a nurse.

Mrs Darling felt sad that he did not get on well with Nana. So she told him about the strange boy who had come in and gone out at the window, and how Nana had tried to seize the boy, but only got hold of his shadow.

"Pooh! Nonsense!" said Mr Darling; but when he was shown the shadow, he left off saying "Nonsense!" It was not a very odd shadow; but, of course, being left wrapped up in a drawer had made it stranger. While Mr Darling was looking at it, Nana returned to give Michael his cough medicine, carrying the bottle and the spoon in her mouth.

Michael said that he wouldn't take it. He said the same thing every night. Nana waited patiently.

"Come, be a man, Michael," said his father.

"Won't," replied Michael. This was his pet word.

"I will fetch you a chocolate to take after it," said Mrs Darling, and she left the room.

"You shouldn't pamper him," cried Mr Darling; and he went on: "Michael, when I was a little boy I took medicine without all this fuss. I said, 'Thank you, dear father and mother, for giving me stuff to make me well.' And the medicine I have to take is much, much nastier than yours. I would take it now, just to show you, only the bottle is lost."

"Oh, I know where it is!" cried Wendy, who was in her nightgown. And in another minute she was back with Mr Darling's proper dose, in a glass.

Mr Darling really hated taking it, and he made

all sorts of excuses. He said he should be sick, and there was a lot more in his glass than Michael's, and so on. Michael said, "Father must take his first," and when Mr Darling said, "No, Michael first," Michael said, "Father's a cowardy custard."

"Why don't both of you take it at the same time?" said Wendy.

"All right," said Mr Darling. Then Wendy counted three, and Michael swallowed his medicine, but Mr Darling hid his own glass behind him. He didn't know what to do with the stuff, and he couldn't be made to drink it, so he poured it into Nana's bowl. He pretended this was great fun. The children watched him in silence. When Nana came in again, he told her: "Good dog, Nana, I have put some milk into your bowl." And indeed, it looked like milk; but when Nana tasted it, she knew he had played a trick on her. She went into her kennel, shedding tears, and had to be cuddled and comforted; so, directly after, had the three children.

For Mr Darling, who knew he was in the

wrong, made things worse by being very cross with Nana. "I won't have a dog in the nursery!" he shouted. "I shall tie her up in the back yard." And he did so. Just fancy, tying up your nurse in the yard!

Poor Nana could not think why she should be treated like that. She whined, for it was snowing off and on; and by and by she barked, for she could smell some sort of danger in the air. Mrs Darling heard these noises while she put the children to bed and lit their night-lights. Wendy, John and Michael fell asleep while she was still singing to them. She felt uneasy at leaving them alone, but there did not seem any harm likely to happen. Besides, the party where she was going was only a few doors away, at No. 27. Still, she would have been glad to stay at home by the three little heads in the three little beds.

She looked out at the stars – there seemed a great many more than usual, and much nearer, too, as if they wanted to peep inside the house. Then she went off with Mr Darling. Neither of them felt the least bit partyish. They crossed the road to No. 27.

And as soon as these grown-up people were well out of the way, the stars became wildly excited, and could be heard (if anybody had been listening) calling out: "Hi! Peter! Hurry up! Come along, Peter!"

3

Peter, Wendy, and a Thimble

Now it was all dark and quiet in the little Darlings' room, for the three night-lights went out almost as soon as Mrs Darling did.

But it was only dark for a moment, for a bright light flew in at the window (the top of which was open) and rushed to and fro like a ball of quicksilver. If this light had ever stood still, it would be been seen for what it was – a lovely little-girl fairy, called Tinker

Bell. She was darting all round the room hunting for Peter's shadow. But that was folded up in a drawer, you know, and she never thought of looking there. She was too busy searching in pockets and behind pictures. She even peered into a jug: it was empty, and she dropped into it to see what it was like. It was the first time she had ever been in a jug in her life. She did enjoy it!

So her light was hidden when Peter himself came in at the window. He guessed where she was. "Oh Tink, do come out of that jug!" he called softly. "And tell me, have you found where they put my shadow?"

She answered him in a voice like a tiny bell with a silvery tinkle, which is the fairy language. It was the only way she could speak, and that's why she was named Tinker Bell. Peter knew what she meant, though nobody else could have understood. She said that his shadow was somewhere in the big box – she meant the chest of drawers. It was too big for her to open. Peter had his shadow out in a second, and was so excited at getting it back

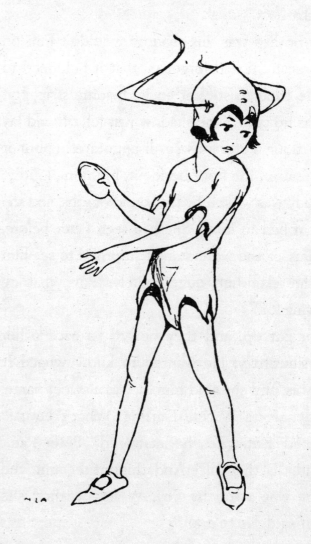

that he shut Tinker Bell in the drawer and never noticed.

The bother was, his shadow wouldn't join on to him again. It had forgotten that it belonged to him. He tried to stick it on with some soap, but that was no good. The shadow just fell off and lay on the floor. Peter was so disappointed about it that he sat on the floor beside it, blubbing loudly.

Wendy was woken by the sound of sobs, and she sat up in bed to listen. She had seen Peter before, in dreams, so she was not a bit surprised to see him now. She asked him, quite politely, "Boy, what are you crying for?"

Peter got up, and they bowed to each other most beautifully. He wanted to know what her name was, and she told him. It was a sweet name: "Wendy Moira Angela Darling. What's yours?" she asked. But when he answered, "Peter Pan," she said, "Is that all?" And this rather annoyed him; he was a touchy boy. Wendy wished she had not said, "Is that all?"

"Where do you live?" she went on. Peter

answered, "Second turn to the right, and then straight on till morning." Wendy nearly said, "Is that all?" again, but she was too polite. She looked at Peter, and saw how prettily he was dressed, in leaves sewn together; some of the leaves, however, were coming undone. She was just going to offer to fix them up for him, when he began to explain why he was crying. It was because he could not get his shadow to stick on. So Wendy fetched her needle and cotton and thimble, and sewed the shadow on to Peter's foot; she hurt him as little as she could help. When he found that it was now safely stuck on, he danced about and crowed with joy. For, to tell the truth, Peter was very conceited. And instead of saying, "Thank you, Wendy, how kind you are!" he crowed, "Oh, how clever I am!"

Wendy was offended, and no wonder. She went back to bed, and Peter had to come and beg her pardon before she would even peep out from under the blankets. But she was a good, forgiving little girl, and by and by she sat beside Peter on the side of the bed and said, "If you like, I will give you a kiss."

Peter held his hand out.

"Surely you know what a kiss is!" said Wendy.

"I shall know when you give it to me," Peter answered.

Wendy did not want his feelings to be hurt any more, so she took off her thimble and gave him that. It was a nice little silver one. Peter liked the thimble so much that he offered to give Wendy a kiss. She turned her face towards him, and he gave her an acorn button off his coat. It was not the sort of kiss she cared about, but she said she would always wear it on the chain round her neck. After all, she could not expect everyone to know as much about kissing as Mrs Darling did. Especially Peter, who, Wendy soon found out, had no mother.

"No mother?" Wendy was shocked.

"Don't have a mother," said Peter. "Don't want one. What use would a mother be to me?"

"How old are you?" Wendy asked him.

"Don't know," said Peter.

"If you did have a mother, at any rate you could ask her how old you were. *She* would know," said Wendy.

"She *might*," said Peter. "But you see, Wendy, I ran away the day I was born!"

"Oooh!" exclaimed Wendy. "What a silly thing to do!"

"Not at all," replied Peter. "I heard my father and mother talking about what I was to be when I was a grown-up man. And I don't want to be grown-up! I won't be grown-up! I want always to be a little boy and to have fun."

"Oooh!" cried Wendy again. "But how can you do that?"

Peter explained that he had flown right away to Kensington Gardens the day he was born, and had lived a long time among the fairies. And they had told him lots of things. "So I am now very wise," he ended. (But that was really only his conceitedness.) "Yes, Wendy, I believe I am so wise and so clever that I shall never grow up at all if I don't choose!"

Wendy did not feel so sure about the wiseness

and cleverness as Peter did. But she loved him ever so much already. And when he said that he had lived with the fairies, she *was* surprised! "What!" she said. "Do you really know some fairies?"

"Oh, lots and lots!" said Peter.

"How splendid!" said Wendy.

"Well, yes, perhaps," said Peter. "But they are rather a bother, you know. They get in one's way so. Indeed, sometimes I have to spank them." Then Wendy asked so many questions that he could hardly answer her fast enough. She wanted to know, "Who *are* the fairies, really and truly? Where do they come from? What do they live on? Where would one be likely to find any? Would they let me speak to them?" and so on.

"Well, it's like this," said Peter. "When the first baby that ever was laughed for the first time that ever was —"

"What was the baby's name?" asked Wendy.

"Don't interrupt. I don't know. Anyhow, its laugh broke up into a thousand little tiny pieces, and they all went skipping about, and turned into fairies."

"Were you there?" said Wendy.

"Don't interrupt. No I wasn't. But there are only a few fairies now, because children don't believe in them. They can't live unless they're believed in. And every time a child says, 'I don't believe there are such things as fairies,' then another fairy falls down dead."

"Oh, dear!" said Wendy. "How very sad!"

"Goodness me!" said Peter suddenly. "I wonder where – Tink! Tink! Tink!" he called. "Where are you?" To tell the truth, he had quite forgotten her. "I can't think where she has gone to," he said uneasily; and he got up and began to hunt about.

"Oh Peter!" cried Wendy. "Surely there isn't a fairy in this room?"

"She was here just now – but she is keeping very quiet," replied Peter. "Listen, Wendy, listen hard. Do you hear anything?"

"I hear a sound like a tinkle of little tiny bells," said Wendy. "It seems to come from the chest of drawers."

"Why, that's Tink!" said Peter. "That's the fairy

language. Oh, Wendy, I do believe I've shut her up in the drawer!" And he gurgled with laughter.

"Poor little thing! You must let her out at once!" cried Wendy.

Peter opened the drawer where the tinkle was, and Tinker Bell flew out.

"You silly boy!" she screamed at Peter, and darted all round the nursery, shrieking with rage.

Peter said he was sorry, but how could he know she was in the drawer?

"Oh Peter," cried Wendy, "if only she would stop still a minute! I can't see her properly."

"Fairies are like that," said Peter. "They hardly ever stand still." But just then Tink settled for a moment on the top of the cuckoo clock, and glared at Wendy. Tink looked quite ugly with the temper she was in; but Wendy exclaimed, "Oh, how lovely!"

"Tink, the lady would like to have you for her fairy," said Peter. He thought this would please Tink, and soothe her down. But she answered very rudely. Wendy did not understand the fairy language, so Peter had to explain.

"She says you are a great ugly girl, and she doesn't want to be your fairy; she wants to be mine."

Wendy did not like this.

"But you know you can't really be my fairy, Tink," he continued, "because I'm a gentleman and you are not."

"You silly boy!" answered Tink, and she flew into the bathroom.

"You mustn't mind her," said Peter to Wendy. "She is a rude, common little fairy. She mends the pots and kettles – that's why she's called Tinker Bell."

This was not the real reason at all, but Peter had a bad habit of saying the first thing that came into his head. He was now sitting with Wendy in the big arm-chair. She went on asking him more questions.

"Where do you live now, Peter? Are you in Kensington Gardens still?"

"Sometimes," he said, "but mostly I live in the Never-Land along with the Lost Boys."

"Are they fairies?"

"No; they are the children who fall out of their prams when their nurses aren't watching them. Then the fairies pick them up and take care of them for seven days to see if anybody comes for them. If not, they are sent away to the Never-Land. And I am their captain."

"But why are they all boys?"

"Because girls are too clever to fall out of their prams."

This remark pleased Wendy so much that she said: "You can give me a kiss."

"I thought you would want it back," said Peter rather crossly, and he held out the thimble.

"Oh dear, I don't mean that," she said; and she thought, "If he calls a thimble a kiss, I had better call a kiss a thimble."

"I meant a thimble," she told him. "Like this." And she kissed him.

"How funny!" said Peter. "Shall I give you a thimble like that?" He did so; it was rather pecky. But, straight after, Wendy screeched. For Tinker

Bell was pulling her hair, and darting to and fro in a worse temper than ever. And when Peter tried to quiet her, she only answered sharply: "You silly boy!" Certainly Tink was no lady.

4

The Children Escape

It was beautifully light in the nursery, for Wendy had turned the light up when she was sewing Peter's shadow on. She and he were still sitting, all comfy and cosy, in the big arm-chair, and the next thing Wendy wanted to know was why he was so fond of coming to the window? She thought, of course, it was to see her, perhaps to get a little sewing and mending done. But she was quite mistaken.

Peter was a truthful person, and rather a

heartless one too. So he told her (though he could see she was disappointed) he came to listen to stories – the stories Mrs Darling told the children at bedtime.

He said, "You see, I don't know any stories. No more do any of the Lost Boys. Nobody ever told us any."

Wendy thought that was perfectly awful. Peter went on: "So I come here to pick up any odds and ends of stories I can. The bother is, I never hear them right through to the end. Oh, Wendy, your mother was telling you such a beautiful story last time I came."

"What was it about?"

"About a prince who couldn't find a lady who wore a glass slipper."

"Oh, Peter!" said Wendy, quite excited. "That was the story of Cinderella! And the prince *did* find her in the end, and they lived happily ever after."

Peter was very pleased to hear this. He jumped up and rushed to the window. Wendy cried,

"Wherever are you going?"

"Why, to tell the other boys."

"Oh, no, Peter, don't go yet!" said Wendy. "I know lots of other stories. Oh, what heaps of stories I could tell you!"

Peter came back with a greedy look in his eyes. "Come along!" he ordered. He gripped hold of Wendy and began pulling her towards the window.

"Let me go!" said Wendy, wriggling.

"But I want you to come back with me and tell us stories. You could be a sort of mother for us," said Peter.

Wendy was pleased at being asked, but she replied: "Oh, but I can't. Whatever would Mummy say? And I can't fly, either."

"I'll teach you," said Peter. "We just jump on the back of the wind, that's all, and away we go."

"Oooh, how lovely!"

"And you could go on flying about among the stars with me, instead of being asleep on a silly bed. Such fun! And when we get to the Never-Land, there are mermaids, and fairies, and—" Peter was going to say pirates, but he thought it better not to mention them. He had an idea that girls were easily frightened. So he went on: "Yes, Wendy, you could tuck us in at night, the way your mother does; and darn our stockings; and tell us all the stories we have never heard. Oh, it would be splendid!"

"Oooh," said Wendy. "Yes, of course it would be splendid. But would you teach Michael and John to fly, so that they could come too?"

"If you like," said Peter, who didn't care about Michael and John.

So Wendy shook her brothers and woke them up. "Peter Pan is here," she cried, "and he is going to teach us to fly!"

The two boys were wide-awake in a moment, but Peter made a sign to them to be silent. John cried: "Turn out the light!" They listened in the dark; there wasn't a sound to be heard. Even Nana, who had been barking miserably all evening, was quite quiet now. But Peter, whose ears were very sharp, heard footsteps in the distance.

It was like this. Nana's barking had so much

annoyed the little maid Liza, who was mixing Christmas puddings in the kitchen, that she got muddled between the suet and the sugar, the raisins and the currants, and put too much of one thing and too little of another. At last she became very cross, and she fetched Nana indoors and took her upstairs to the nursery. "There, you silly!" she said to Nana. "You see there's nothing at all to bark about. They are all breathing sweetly in their beds." But Liza little knew that the sweet breathing was behind the window-curtains, where the three children and Peter were hiding.

"Now then, Nana, no more of this nonsense!" said Liza severely. "If you bark any more, I shall go and fetch master and missus from the party, and then you'll catch it!" She took Nana away.

"That's all right," said John coming out from behind the window-curtains. "I say, Peter, how *do* you fly?" Peter flew gracefully round the room, to show how easy it was.

"How splendid!" cried the boys. "How sweet!" said Wendy.

"Yes, I *am* sweet!" said Peter in his conceited way.

They tried to imitate him, but they couldn't fly a bit, until Peter blew some fairy dust on each of them. He told them, "All you do is to think lovely, wonderful thoughts, and wriggle your shoulders, and let go."

They found the lovely, wonderful thoughts rather a bother – you can't think any, all of a sudden, like that but they wriggled and let go, and the fairy dust did the rest. In half a minute the three little Darlings were fluttering round and round the room, with their heads bobbing against the ceiling. It was glorious! And when John found he really could fly, and that there were pirates in the Never-Land, he made up his mind he must see them. There was no time to lose. He seized his Sunday hat – it looked rather funny along with night-clothes! – and cried, "Let's be off at once!"

"Yes, let's!" cried everybody else.

The stars, who were watching and waiting to see what would happen, immediately blew the window open.

Meanwhile, it was about ten minutes since Nana had been fastened up in the yard. She was sure there was something wrong in the nursery – she could feel that her dear little charges were in danger, and yet what could she do? It was no good barking; that was quite plain. So she went on pulling and straining at her chain with all her might and main. And at last it broke.

Mr and Mrs Darling were horrified to see her bursting into where they were at the party, dragging her broken chain and throwing up her paws. They left No. 27 in a fright, and followed Nana into the street.

Just fancy how startled and shocked they were when they looked up at their own nursery window and saw that the room was full of light, and that there were three – no, four – shadows on the curtain; shadows of little figures flying round and round, up and down, to and fro. Yes, *flying*! Goodness me! Were they dreaming, or what? They were trembling with fear as they opened the street door, and ran upstairs as softly as possible. They might perhaps have been in time if they had gone faster. Perhaps – but I don't think so.

And as they reached the nursery door, Nana gave a great sad howl. For she could hear things better than Mr and Mrs Darling. And somehow she knew that the window had opened just that minute, and four little people had gone flying out into the night.

Tinker Bell made five, of course; but we will not count her, because she was so small and so disagreeable.

5

The Fly-by-Nights

The way to the Never-Land was very much longer than Wendy, John and Michael had ever thought. Peter, who said anything that came handy, had made Wendy believe it was as easy as anything to get there: just "second to the right, and straight on till morning."

Well it *may* have been "second to the right," but it certainly wasn't straight on after that. Peter took the children such a roundabout way, and stopped so often to look at things, that a lot of time was lost soon after they started.

Of course it was great fun to be really flying, to be able to go round church steeples or high chimneys, just as if one were a swallow. But it's rather shivery in nighties. And when there had been darks and lights, and days and nights, and seas and lands, without getting anywhere in particular, the little Darlings very nearly wished they hadn't come.

They were so hungry, but there was nothing to eat; and they were so sleepy, but there was no nice bed to snuggle into. They couldn't help shutting their eyes sometimes as they flew; and if they shut their eyes, they dropped down at once – generally over the sea. This happened rather often to Michael, because he was the youngest and the sleepiest. He would go falling like a stone toward the water, and Wendy would cry, "Save him, save him!" and just as he was almost in the sea, Peter would dive down and catch him. Not because he was sorry for Michael, but just to show how clever he was. Peter thought it was all great fun, watching the children fluttering along while he shot up to the stars and down to the waves, and showed-off all the cleverness he knew.

Sometimes he went out of sight for quite a long while, and they had to fly without a guide as best they could. And when he *did* come back, he had nearly forgotten who they were, and indeed Wendy had once to tell him her name. It was rather lonely, being left alone in the air like this, and they kept on bumping up against clouds.

But nobody liked to say anything to blame Peter, because, if he were to get cross with them, and perhaps fly away, how would they reach the Never-Land at all?

Still, you may be sure they were very, very glad when, one evening, after they had been flying ever so long, Peter suddenly said, "There it is!"

"Where, where?"

"Where all the arrows are pointing."

The arrows were the rays of the setting sun. They lit up the whole island. The children knew it at once. They felt as if they had come back home there to a happy, friendly place. For they could see all the different things they had made-believe about. The lagoon was there, and John's flamingo, and Michael's cave, and Wendy's wolf. Indeed, the children seemed to know as much about the island as Peter did: there was nothing he could tell them. This rather annoyed him.

But just as they were joyfully calling out to each other, "There's my boat!" "There's the Redskin camp!" "Look at the turtles!" and so on – the sun sank and the Never-Land grew dark. It grew darker every moment. It didn't look happy or friendly any longer. And the children felt frightened; anybody would be, who was used to going to sleep with night-lights. For there were no night-lights here, no nursery, no Nana – no dear, delightful Mrs Darling. There were only themselves and Peter – who might very likely leave them in the dark, just for fun.

They were flying over the island now, so low that sometimes their feet touched the tree-tops.

They kept as close to Peter as they could. And the horrid part was they felt as if somebody or something was trying to stop them, so that they had to push their way, yet there was nothing to be seen. Peter, who seemed very gay and cheerful, said: "They don't want us to land." Who could "they" be?

By and by he wanted to know which they would rather have first – an adventure, or tea? Wendy and Michael wanted tea, but John thought he would like the adventure, until he found out what sort of adventure it was. Peter said there was a pirate asleep in the grass just beneath them, and if John liked, they could go down and kill him.

John, however, could not see the pirate, and thought it would be best to have tea first. He asked:

"Are there many pirates on the Island now?"

"Never known so many," said Peter.

"Who is their captain?"

Peter looked very grave and stern as he answered with one word:

"Hook."

"Not James Hook?"

"Yes."

This was dreadful. Michael began to cry, and John had a nasty dry feeling in his throat. For they had heard of James Hook. Even in the peacefulness of their nursery, and the quiet of the Kindergarten, the name of Hook made people very uneasy. There was no pirate, alive or dead, quite so terrible as Hook. And now they were, as you may say, nearly face to face with him! He was the last man they had ever expected to meet.

"What is he like?" said John, with a gulp. "Is he big?"

"Not so big as he was."

"How do you mean?"

"I cut off a bit of him."

"You!"

"Yes, me," said Peter, rather snappishly.

"I didn't mean to be rude," said John.

"Oh, all right."

"But, what bit did you cut off?"

"His right hand."

John cheered up on hearing this, and said: "Then he can't fight now?"

Peter replied: "Oh, can't he just? He has an iron hook now instead of a hand, and he claws with it."

Everybody turned pale.

"Now, John, look here."

"Yes."

"Say, 'Aye, aye, sir!'" said Peter sharply.

John was feeling so serious about Hook that he said "Aye, aye, sir," as meek as a mouse.

"Every boy who serves under me," said Peter, "has got to promise one thing. So must you. It's this. If we meet Hook in an open fight, you must leave him to me. Don't go at him yourself."

"Aye, aye, sir," said John. "I promise."

Meanwhile, Tinker Bell was lighting their way quite nicely, by going round and round them as they flew. They could not see much of the island below them, but they could see Peter and each other.

Peter stopped every minute or two and listened

(he could poise in the air like a bird), staring down through the darkness. Then he would go on again, without explaining anything. This made the children rather uneasy, but they thought he must know what he was doing.

By and by he suddenly said: "Tink tells me the pirates sighted us before it was dark."

"Oh dear!"

"And they have got out their big gun, Long Tom. They can see Tink's light, of course, and they are likely to let fly, because they know we must be near it."

"Oh, Wendy!"

"Oh, John!"

"Oh, Michael!"

"Oh, Peter!" they all three cried. "Do tell her to go away!"

Peter replied that he certainly would not. "She is frightened," he said. "She thinks we have lost the way."

Wendy said: "Then tell her to put her light out."

"She can't. It never goes out unless she's asleep."

John cried: "Then tell her to go to sleep."

"She can't. A fairy can't sleep unless she's sleepy."

This made things very difficult.

"If only one of us had a pocket to carry her in," said Peter. But nobody had. Pockets are very seldom put in nighties, and never in skeleton leaves, like Peter's suit. Then Peter remembered John's top hat. Tink did not object to being put into that. So it was first carried by John, and afterwards by Wendy. And Tink's light was so completely hidden, nobody could have known she was there.

It was very dark without her, though. And everything was so still (except for a few strange sounds which could well have been done without) that the children found it darker and lonelier than ever. They went on flying through the silent night, and at last Michael whimpered that he didn't like it being so lonely. He said: "If only something would make some noise!"

It did. There was a most enormous *bang*, which echoed like a roaring lion all around them. The pirates had fired Long Tom, on the chance of hitting Peter or someone. And this explosion did a lot of harm, for it scattered all the children away from each other. John and Michael found themselves all alone; Peter was blown out to sea; Wendy was blown upwards, carrying Tinker Bell in the hat.

It was a pity Wendy did not drop the hat. For Tink, who hated her, at once came out of it, and tried to get rid of Wendy. Tink could only be one thing at a time, either all bad, or all good. Just at present she was all bad. She tinkled most beautifully at Wendy as she flew to and fro. Wendy, who was so kind herself that she never dreamed of anybody wanting to hurt her, thought that Tink was offering to show her the way.

"Peter!" cried Wendy. "John! Michael! Where ever are you? Do answer!" But everything was silent.

There was only Tinker Bell to help her. So she followed that deceitful tinkle.

6

The Never-Land

The people of the Never-Land had a feeling that Peter would soon be home again. So they began to wake up and get ready for him, so that when he came he might find them all very busy.

You see, while he was away, they always kept quiet. Nobody bothered to fight anybody else. But

Peter liked things to be exciting; so now things had to be made exciting as fast as possible.

There were six sorts of people who lived in the Island. (1) The Fairies – mostly high up in nests, in tall tree-tops. (2) The Mermaids, in the lagoon – mostly deep down under water. (3) The Wild Beasts – whose dens were in the woods and mountains. (4) The Redskins Indians who camped anywhere they chose. (5) The Pirates – who returned every night to their brig *The Jolly Roger*. (6) The Lost Boys – whose home, a very nice one, was underground, as you will hear.

All these were enemies, except the Fairies and the Mermaids, who kept well out of the way. And in the evening, when Peter and the little Darlings got there, everybody was moving round and round the Island after each other, very fierce.

It was a great change from their peace -and quiet. While Peter was away, the Redskins had been having a large greedy feast for six days and nights, the Wild Beasts had been attending to their young ones, and the Pirates and Lost Boys, if they happened to meet, merely bit their thumbs at each other and passed on.

But the Islanders could make themselves fierce all in a minute. And now they were moving on each other's track, slowly and silently. The Lost Boys were looking for Peter, their captain, whom they expected back any minute. The Pirates were looking for the Lost Boys. The Redskins were hunting the Pirates; and the Wild Beasts were prowling after the Redskins.

The Lost Boys, instead of being slim and graceful like Peter in his skeleton-leaf-suit, were dressed in the skins of bears which they had killed. They were almost round, like balls of fur – indeed, they were so round that if they fell they rolled about. So they had to be careful *not* to fall. Each wore a dagger, and they crept along very softly, one by one, looking as if they were saying "Hush!"

There were six of them. Tootles, who was kind and brave, but always unlucky; Nibs, a light-hearted boy; and Slightly, the most conceited of them all. Next came Curly, a regular pickle, and the Twins, who had no names, because they got lost before their mother had made up her mind what to call them. These Boys were quite unlike each other (except for the bearskins), but most of all they were unlike Peter. Indeed, Peter had forbidden them to look the least bit like him.

But as soon as the Lost Boys had gone on into

the dark, there came a gang of ugly ruffians – the ugliest ever were seen. Before they were in sight, their horrid voices could be heard, bawling a verse of their favourite song. This was it:

> *"Avast belay, yo ho, heave to,*
> *A-pirating we go,*
> *And if we're parted by a shot,*
> *We're sure to meet below!"*

The most dreadful lot of Pirates they were. How many, I cannot say, but some of the worst of them were an Italian, named Cecco, and a huge man generally called the Blackamoor, because that's what he was, and Smee the bo'sun, and Gentleman Starkey, and Bill Jukes, and Skylights. They were covered with scars and tattoo marks – with pistols, cutlasses, daggers, knives, muskets, and many other cutting and shooting things.

The Pirate Captain, James Hook, lay smoking two cigars at once, in a sort of chariot which his men moved along. If they did not go quick enough, he frightened them by shaking his iron claw, or hook. They obeyed him as if they were dogs, because they were so afraid of being clawed. He was a strange-looking man, with long black curls and very polite manners. He had never been known to show any fear in his life – unless he caught sight of his own blood, which was a very ugly colour. But this hardly ever happened.

The Pirates passed, making their hideous noise, and a few minutes afterwards the Redskins followed. If you had not seen the Pirates first, you would have wanted to run away from the Redskins. They wore no clothes, but were well oiled all over, and their eyes glittered in the dark. Their chief was called Great Big Little Panther. He went in front, on all fours, so that he might look more like a panther; but as he, and the whole of his tribe, had just been munching frightfully, he was feeling much too fat. The only person who had not over-eaten was the beautiful princess, Tiger-Lily. She walked last of all, very proud and upright.

The Redskins stole out of sight, and very soon

the Wild Beasts appeared, an enormous number of them – dreadful creatures with large teeth showing and red tongues hanging out. Lions, tigers, bears, and other big animals – and a lot of smaller beasts, all savage and all hungry.

When these had gone by, there was still one more to pass; it had not been mentioned before. It came, making curious noises as it crept along. It was a large, a *very* large, Crocodile.

There was nobody after the Crocodile, because the Lost Boys did not know it was there. They appeared again presently, having gone right round the Island. They were tired, and lay down on the turf, which indeed was the roof of their underground home. And every one of them said: "I do wish Peter would come back!" They meant, to keep the Pirates off.

Slightly said in his conceited way: "I am the only one who is not afraid of the Pirates!" But directly after, he repeated that he wished Peter *would* come back.

The Lost Boys, who were feeling lonely, began

to talk about their mothers. They could only do this when Peter was away, because he thought mothers were silly. However, the Lost Boys would have liked some mothers to look after them just then. And while they talked, there was a distant sound. They knew it much too well; it was the Pirate song, getting closer.

The Lost Boys disappeared at once – all except Nibs, who went to watch out for the Pirates. How did they hide so quickly? Why, close to where they lay were seven large hollow trees – a tree for each boy and one for Peter. These were the secret stairs and doorways to the delightful home under the ground. Hook had no notion where to find it. But now here was Hook himself, the moment after, with his horrible Pirate crew. They caught sight of Nibs scuttling among the trees, and Hook sent them to search for the other Boys. He was left alone with his bosun, Smee, and he began to tell Smee the story of his life. Smee did not understand it in the least, but Hook went on speaking.

"Most of all," said Hook, "I hate Peter Pan. It was

he who cut off my arm and threw it to a Crocodile. And the Crocodile liked my arm so much, Smee, that it has followed me everywhere since, wanting the rest of me!"

"I have often noticed," said Smee, "that you were oddly afraid of crocodiles."

"Only that one crocodile. It's waiting, I tell you, for the rest of me. And I'm waiting to get hold of Peter Pan!" As Hook spoke, he sat down upon a large mushroom. "But listen, Smee, that crocodile once swallowed a clock, and the clock goes *tick*, *tick*, *tick* inside it. So I can hear it coming along, and I have time to get away!"

Smee answered that some day the clock must stop. "And then," said he, "the Crocodile will get you."

Hook was just saying that he knew that, when he suddenly jumped up. He cried: "Why, this mushroom is hot! I'm nearly burning!" And he and the bosun tried, very gingerly, to pull the mushroom up. It came up at once, for it had no root. There was a hole where it had been, and smoke came out of the hole. No wonder Hook felt hot! The mushroom was the stopper of the Lost Boys' chimney. And the two Pirates could hear the Lost Boys chattering gaily down below.

The home under the ground had been found at last! And soon Hook noticed the seven hollow trees. He stood thinking for a long time, making a plan to trap the Lost Boys, while Peter was away. He told Smee what it was – like this:

"We will go back to the ship and cook a large rich cake, with green sugar on it. We will leave the cake on the shore of the Mermaids' Lagoon. And when the boys come to play with the Mermaids, they will find it. They have no mother, so they don't know it is dangerous to eat rich, damp cake. And so they will gobble it up, and they will die! Ha! ha! ha!"

Hook and Smee laughed and danced with joy at the thought of this wicked plan. And they began to sing the Pirates' song; but they heard a little wee sound they stopped to listen. Yes, it certainly was—

Tick, tick, tick, tick!

It was the Crocodile.

Hook ran away in a terrible fright. Smee was not so frightened, because the Crocodile was not coming after *him*. But he ran away too.

The Lost Boys, little thinking that their enemies had been listening down their chimney, came up into the open air again. Nibs was not there, but directly afterwards he rushed up to them. A pack of wolves was close behind, baying and hanging out their tongues at Nibs. He fell upon the ground, and cried: "Save me! Save me!"

That was easier said than done. The boys had to think as fast as anything, because the wolves were not waiting to think at all. They said to each other, "What would Peter do? Why, Peter would look at them through his legs." And they bent double and went backwards at the wolves, looking at them through their legs.

The wolves saw five pairs of eyes looking angrily at them upside down, and they were so worried that they fled.

When Nibs had got his breath back, he said: "I have seen a wonderful thing. There's a great white bird flying this way. And as it flies it moans, 'Poor Wendy!'"

"There *are* birds, I remember, called Wendies," said Slightly. He always pretended to remember

things in England before he got lost and was taken to the Island.

"There it is, coming now!" cried Curly. They could see Wendy flying overhead, and heard her sad cries. Tinker Bell was pinching her all over. Tink's light was flashing to and fro, and she was making a shrill tinkle.

The Boys were very much puzzled. They shouted: "Hallo, Tink!"

And the naughty little thing replied: "Peter wants you to shoot the Wendy."

They rushed down underground to fetch their bows and arrows, all except Tootles, who had his with him.

"Quick, quick, Tootles!" screamed Tink. "Peter will be so pleased."

"Get out of the way, Tink," shouted Tootles; and he shot up at Wendy.

Wendy fluttered to the ground with an arrow in her breast.

7

The Little House is Built

When the five other boys came back with their bows and arrows, they found Wendy lying on the ground, and Tootles ever so pleased with himself. He cried, "You are too late. I have shot the Wendy!"

They did not hear Tinker Bell saying "Silly boy!" as she flew away to hide. Tootles had done exactly what she wanted, and he would get all the blame.

The Boys crowded round Wendy, and Slightly was (as usual) the first to speak. He said in a frightened voice: "But this is not a bird. I think it's a lady." Tootles began to tremble. *Could* it be a lady?

"Then we have killed her," said Nibs.

"I see what it is," said Curly. "Peter was bringing us a lady."

"Yes, a lady who would take care of us," said the twins, "and now Tootles has shot her."

Tootles was very pale. He said that he had never

seen a lady except in dreams, and then he called her Pretty Mother. "But when a real lady came," he went on sadly, "I shot her."

They all were thinking the same thought: "Oh, won't Peter be angry!" And Tootles said he should go away; he was so afraid of Peter.

But now they heard Peter crowing loudly overhead, and the next moment he dropped down beside them. They were all, except Tootles, standing close round the body of Wendy, hoping Peter would not see it.

"I am back again," said Peter. "Why don't you cheer?"

They tried to cheer, but no sound came out of their mouths.

"I have brought you a mother at last," said Peter joyfully. He expected them to say, "How clever you are!" But they didn't.

Peter became rather anxious. He said: "She flew this way. Haven't you seen her?"

"Peter," said Tootles. "I will show her to you. Get back, twins – let Peter see."

Peter looked at Wendy lying there with the arrow still sticking in her. He did not know what to say or to do. After some time he remarked that Wendy was dead. "Perhaps she is frightened at being dead," he went on. He thought of making a joke out of it, and hopping off on one leg. I told you Peter was quite heartless. But somebody ought to be punished. So he took the arrow out of Wendy's breast, and asked whose was it?

Tootles bravely answered that it was his. Peter was then going to stab him with it – and Tootles, kneeling, waited to be killed; he was sure he deserved it. But somehow Peter could not make up his mind to kill Tootles. And while the rest were watching him in wonder, Nibs was watching Wendy. He cried: "The Wendy lady moved her arm! I heard her say, 'Poor Tootles!'"

Peter said: "Then she is alive."

"The Wendy lady is alive!" shouted Slightly.

Peter knelt by her, and found that the button he had given her, which she had put upon the chain round her neck, had saved her life. The arrow had struck against it. Wendy was not dead. She was only fainting.

"Do get better quickly, Wendy," said Peter. "I want to show you the Mermaids." But of course she could not answer. What was that curious noise overhead?

"Listen to Tink," said Curly. "She is crying because she wanted the Wendy to be killed."

Peter did not know what this meant, but when they told him how Tink had screamed at them to shoot the Wendy, he was shocked and said: "Tink, I will not be your friend any more. Go away for ever."

Tink begged and prayed, but Peter would not listen, until he saw Wendy move her arm again, and then he said: "Well, go away for a whole week, anyhow." And Tink flew away, as cross as two sticks.

Peter and the boys were wondering what to do with the fainting Wendy. Curly said: "Let us carry her down into our house," and Slightly agreed that this was the proper way to behave to ladies.

"Oh, no," said Peter, "it would not be respectful to touch her."

"Just what I was thinking," said Slightly.

"But she will die if we leave her here," said Tootles.

"Yes, she will," said Slightly, "but there is nothing else to be done."

"Oh, but there is," cried Peter. "We will build a little house all round her."

Wasn't this a clever plan! Peter made the boys fetch branches, and moss, and furniture from the house underground – as fast as they could go.

And while they were scurrying all over the

place – almost tumbling over each other, they were so eager to please Peter – two sleepy persons crawled in among them. These were John and Michael, who kept on going to sleep, and just waking up enough to take another step, and then going to sleep again.

Peter had quite forgotten them; but when they said, "Hullo, Peter," he began to remember.

They asked, "Is Wendy asleep?"

Peter was busy measuring Wendy, so as to leave some room beside her for a table and chairs. He said "Yes," without thinking.

"Let's waken her to make us some supper," said Michael.

But Peter commanded them to help build Wendy's house. He told Curly to see that they did. John and Michael were so surprised at the idea of building a house for Wendy, that Michael forgot to say "Won't!" – and John forgot to be sleepy. They were at once made to work like anything.

"First we must put the table and chairs and

fender," said Peter. "Then we shall build the house all round them."

"Yes, I remember," said Slightly, "that is the way a house is built."

"Slightly, go and fetch a doctor," said Peter.

"Aye, aye sir," said Slightly. He went away, and returned with John's top-hat on. He made-believe to be a doctor; and, as Peter did not know the difference between real and make-believe, this did very well. Peter called him "sir," and Slightly pretended to put a glass thing in Wendy's mouth. When he took it out again, he told Peter it had cured her. Next, he ordered that she was to be given beef-tea out of a cup with a spout to it. Then he gave back the hat, which was quite real, to John, from whom he had borrowed it without asking.

The odd thing was, that Wendy really *was* getting better. She began to move a little, though her eyes were still shut; and by and by her mouth opened.

"Perhaps she is going to sing in her sleep," said Peter. "Wendy, will you sing what sort of a house you would like?" Wendy then sang a little verse, still with her eyes shut:

> *"I wish I had a pretty house,*
> *The littlest ever seen,*
> *With funny little red walls,*
> *And roof of mossy green."*

They got it made almost at once, because they had all the building stuff ready handy. They sang as they worked; the little house looked so jolly, with red branches and green moss and make-believe roses. Inside it, they had put the nicest things from the house under the ground. And when they thought it was all properly finished, Peter told them they had forgotten the door-knocker and the chimney. So they put the sole of a shoe for a knocker; and John's top-hat, with the bottom taken out, made a splendid chimney, which started smoking at once.

Then they all waited round while Peter knocked at the door. They did so wonder what would happen next!

The door was opened, and out came Wendy. She asked: "Where am I?"

"Wendy lady," said Slightly, "this is the house we have built for you."

"Do say you're pleased!" said Nibs.

"It's a lovely, darling house!" exclaimed Wendy.

The Lost Boys knelt down and held out their arms, and cried: "Oh, Wendy lady, be our mother!"

Wendy was delighted, but she answered that she was only a little girl.

"That won't matter," said Peter. "A nice motherly person is all we want."

"Very well," said Wendy. "I feel that is just what I am. I will do my best. Children, before I put you to bed I will finish the story of Cinderella."

So they all squeezed somehow into the Little House, while Wendy told them stories. And then they were tucked up in bed in their own home under the trees. Wendy was most beautifully motherly. When she had gone to sleep in the Little House, Peter, with his sword drawn, stood and watched outside. Everything was bright and happy as could be. The fairies, going home late, found Peter asleep too: this amused them very much, but did not surprise them. They had got used to Peter by now.

8

All Sorts of Adventures

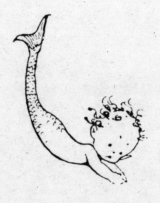

As there was plenty of room in the house underground, Peter ordered that the three little Darlings should live there with the Lost Boys: so Wendy and John and Michael were each given a hollow tree for going down and up again. And they soon learned to go up and down as easily as if they had done it all their lives. The house underground had only one room, but that was very large. There were stout mushrooms to sit on, which grew out of the floor; there was a tree-trunk which did for a table, only it had to be sawed off every day to keep it short enough. The fireplace was a jolly big one, so that Wendy could dry her washing. There was an enormous bed, in which all the boys slept, as close as sardines in a tin; nobody could turn round unless they all turned. Only Michael was hung up in a basket, because Wendy didn't want him to grow up too soon, and the basket made him seem more like a baby. (Wendy herself slept in her own Little House.)

But of course it was rather a plain sort of room: there was nothing at all grand in it, and nothing very beautiful; excepting just one place, a square hole in the wall, about the size of a canary's cage, with a curtain drawn across, and the most charming furniture inside. A mirror, and wash-stand, and chest of drawers, the tiniest ever you saw, and a couch with a bedspread of fruit-blossom. Rugs, and a carpet, and even a chandelier: though the person who lived there lit up the place herself.

You will have guessed by now that this person was Tink. She was very conceited about this exquisite little room of hers. She boasted about it to the other fairies; but nobody was ever invited in.

Wendy was kept very busy, with such a large family to look after. Sewing, and mending, and darning stockings, and cooking for eight boys and herself and Peter, took up a lot of time. Besides, for hours every evening she had to tell all the stories she could remember. But she didn't mind so much work, because she was so extremely happy. She just loved being a mother to so many children. It was the greatest fun for her.

Sometimes, of course, Wendy thought about home, about Mr and Mrs Darling, and Nana; but she was quite easy in her mind about them. She was sure that she and John and Michael could get back again whenever they liked, and that the nursery window would be left open for them to fly in. She was a little bit bothered to see how John and Michael had nearly forgotten their old home already. She wrote out questions on a slate for them to answer, like, "What is the colour of Mother's eyes?" "Which is taller, Father or Mother?" "Describe Mother's party dress," and so on. The other boys wanted to be given these questions, too, and Slightly wrote an answer to every single one, but, of course, it was all wrong. However, John's answers were quite stupid, and Michael was not at all sure whether Wendy wasn't his real mother. By and by, Wendy found herself forgetting too. Time goes very fast in the Never-Land.

Peter did not play in this slate game, partly because he could neither write nor spell, and partly because he thought all mothers silly. There was one of Wendy's stories, about Mrs Darling, which he simply hated, and he went out by himself in a huff whenever this was being told. No one ever knew what happened when Peter was away alone, but it looked as if he were having adventures. There may have been fights with Pirates, or with Grizzly Bears, or with Redskins: Peter sometimes came home with his head bandaged. Still, it was very difficult to tell if his adventures were real ones or make-believe; it was all the same to him.

There were some real adventures, though, most exciting; Wendy knew they were true, because she was in them herself. There was the cake which the Pirates cooked so that the Boys might die after eating it. It was found, time after time, hidden in different places; but Wendy always snatched it away before any boy could so much as nibble at it. So it became quite old and hard, and came in handy for throwing at the Pirates.

And there was the adventure of the Never-Bird whose nest fell out of a tree into the lagoon; but she went on sitting upon her eggs, and Peter commanded that she was not to be disturbed. And there was the adventure of the Large-Leaf, on which Tink and some rude little street-fairies finding Wendy asleep, put her afloat, hoping she would be carried away by the tide. Tink, you see, was just as spiteful as ever. But Wendy awoke and swam back.

However, the adventure of the Mermaids'

Lagoon, I think, was the biggest of all. The Mermaids did not like the Boys coming to play in their lagoon, and they objected so much to Wendy that they would dive at once if they saw her, and splash her with their tails if they possibly could. This was very unfriendly, for Wendy would have liked to talk to them, if it were only a few words about the weather. But they never said a single civil thing to her, not even "Good afternoon," although they would chatter by the hour with Peter.

One summer day the Boys were lying in the sun, dozing, on the great rock called Marooners' Rock. Wendy was wide-awake, stitching away at her needlework. Suddenly the air grew dark and cold, and there came a funny sound, nearer and nearer, across the water. Wendy did not know what it was, but Peter did. It was the noise of muffled oars. Now, nobody but the sly Pirates would use muffled oars. In fact, they were the only people on the Island who had any oars at all.

So when Peter shouted, "Pirates! Dive!" everyone woke up and jumped into the water. Peter and

Wendy stayed together behind the rock, where they were not likely to be seen.

The Pirate dinghy was rowed up to the rock by Smee the bosun and his comrade Starkey, both of them thoroughly bad men. They had taken prisoner the Redskin princess, Tiger-Lily; they had tied her hand and foot, and were going to leave her on the rock to be drowned! This shows how black-hearted they were.

Peter made up his mind to save Tiger-Lily. The easiest thing would have been to wait till the Pirates had gone away again. But Peter did not care for an easy way. He bobbed up and down in the water behind the rock, and imitated the voice of Hook, so cleverly that Smee and Starkey thought it was their captain calling to them. Peter ordered them to set Tiger-Lily free, and let her go. He said he would claw them if they didn't obey at once.

They thought this very odd, but they were afraid to contradict their captain. They cut the cords round Tiger-Lily's arms and legs, and she slipped into the lagoon and swam ashore. Peter and Wendy were delighted at seeing this; and Peter was just about to give one of his most conceited crows, when Wendy put her hand over his mouth. For the real Hook was now shouting over the lagoon, as he swam to the rock. "Boat ahoy!" he cried. The two Pirates showed a lantern, and lighted him, so that he climbed up beside them and sat down, all dismal and dripping, resting his head on his hook. Oh, how he groaned and sighed! Smee and Starkey could not think what was the matter with him; but at last they ventured to ask him: "What's up, captain?"

Hook replied in a hollow voice: "Those boys have found a mother!"

"What is a mother?" asked Smee. He had never been properly taught.

"That is a mother," said Hook, and he pointed to the Never-Bird sitting on her floating nest. "That nest must have fallen into the water, but would the mother desert her eggs? No."

"If she is a mother," said Starkey, "perhaps she is hanging about here to help Peter."

Hook said that was just what he was afraid of.

Smee and Starkey then understood that Peter and the Boys were quite safe, and could come to no harm from wicked Pirate plots, because they had a mother to take care of them. A mother was stronger than the wickedest Pirate. Whatever could be done?

Suddenly Smee said: "Captain! I say! Couldn't we steal away the Boys' mother – and have her for *our* mother?"

"Splendid!" cried Hook. "Yes, we will seize the children and take them to the ship, and drown them all. Then we shall have Wendy for our mother."

"Never!" cried Wendy behind the rock.

The Pirates asked, "What was that?" but there was silence. So they put their hands on Hook's claw, and agreed to do as he had said, and to kidnap Wendy and destroy the others. Nothing could be simpler. The Pirates chuckled horridly in their joy.

At this minute, Hook remembered about Tiger-Lily. "Where is the Princess?"

"We let her go, as you told us," said Smee.

"You let her go!" cried Hook. He was fearfully angry, but when his men explained that his own voice had given the order, he was very uncomfortable indeed. So were they all. Certainly it was very strange that somebody should be imitating Hook like that. A Mermaid could not do it; nor a Redskin; nor a fairy. Hook thought, "Perhaps the person who is mocking me is still somewhere here." So he called out, and Peter answered him, exactly in his own voice. Just like an echo, only he did not say the same words.

"Stranger, who are you?" said Hook.

"I am Captain James Hook of *The Jolly Roger*," replied Peter.

"Then who am I?" said Hook.

"Only a codfish," said the voice.

Hook was very much annoyed. He shouted, "Have you another name?"

This was only a trick and a trap. But Peter was feeling so frightfully conceited that he did not see what Hook was after. And he answered, in his own proper voice, "I have!" Hook went on making guesses; and at last he got as far as this, that the voice belonged to a wonderful boy, who was close by, but could not be seen.

"You can't guess, you can't guess!" crowed Peter. "Do you give it up?"

"Yes, yes!" cried the Pirates.

"Well, then, I am Peter Pan!"

"Take him dead or alive!" screamed Hook.

"Are you ready, Boys?" shouted Peter.

"Aye, aye, sir!" The answer came from different parts of the lagoon.

"Then go for the Pirates!"

And the fight began.

9

Rescued from the Rock

It was a great fight, though a short one. Eight small boys, armed with daggers, and Peter Pan — that makes nine — against three large grown-up Pirates, each of them hung all over with pistols, guns, knives, cutlasses and other dangerous things; and, of course, there was Hook's iron claw, which was the worst of all.

Tootles was wounded, and Wendy was feeling faint. But the rest managed to conquer Smee and Starkey by attacking them from three sides at once. The defeated ruffians fled back to their ship. A pity they could not have been killed, but it is so difficult to fight properly in the water and on slippery rocks.

Meanwhile the Boys all kept the promise they had made to Peter long ago. Not one of them went near Hook. Peter was waiting to meet with Hook, but the Pirate captain was so cunning that there was no chance to get at him, until he climbed up Marooners' Rock to get a breath of air. At the same moment Peter climbed up on the opposite side, and they met, with their faces almost touching.

Peter was just about to stab the captain, when he saw that Hook was lower down the rock than he was. So he held out his hand to help his enemy up, that they might fight fair. And the ill-natured Hook bit him!

Peter's hand was hurt, but his feelings were

much more hurt. It was so very unfair of Hook. Though, of course, you wouldn't expect a man like that to behave nobly. Anyhow, Peter was so taken aback that he was quite helpless. And while he stared at his dreadful enemy, Hook clawed him twice with the iron claw. All seemed lost, for Hook would have finished off the wounded Peter with one more clawing, when—

Tick, tick, tick, tick!

The Crocodile was swarming up the rock.

Hook only just managed to escape. The Boys saw him, white with fear, swimming wildly towards his ship. They would have swum after him and cheered on the Crocodile, but they were rather uneasy because they could not find either Peter or Wendy. After shouting to them all over the lagoon, and getting no answer, they went home in the Pirates' dinghy, which was drifting about by itself.

Peter and Wendy could not answer, because they had both fainted. They were lying on the rock, and the tide was rising fast. It would soon cover the rock.

Soon they were roused by a Mermaid trying to pull Wendy into the water. Peter drew her up again. She did not seem to understand what danger they were in. He showed her that the rock was nearly under water.

"You see," he said, "it is getting smaller and smaller."

"Then we ought to go," said Wendy cheerfully.

"Yes," said Peter, whose wounds were hurting badly.

"Shall we swim or fly, Peter?"

"Do you think you could swim or fly to the Island without me, Wendy?"

Wendy said she was too tired.

Then Peter had to tell her that he was too much wounded to help her. He said, "Hook has clawed me. I can't fly, and I can't swim."

It was quite plain that very soon they would

both be drowned. It simply couldn't be helped.

And while they sat there waiting, with the water rising steadily round them, something light and papery came and brushed against Peter, as if it were saying, "Can I be any use?" It was the tail of a kite.

"It's Michael's kite," said Peter. Michael had made it and lost it some days before.

Peter suddenly thought that it might help them. He caught the tail and pulled the kite to him – quite a big one it was.

"It could lift Michael," he said. "Why can't it carry you, Wendy?"

"Both of us, Peter."

"No, it can't carry two – I know, because Michael and Curly tried together."

Wendy said she wouldn't go without him. But Peter tied the tail round her, said "Goodbye, Wendy," and pushed her off the rock. The kite soared up in the air; it did not seem to mind Wendy's weight one bit. In a few minutes she was out of sight, and Peter was alone on what was left

above water of the rock. It was a very small bit now; only just room for his feet.

The moon rose, and the lagoon grew lighter. The Mermaids came up from their coral caves and sang sweet, sad songs to the moon, but they never noticed Peter standing there all lonely-proudy. For just one minute he felt – well, sort of rather afraid, you know, for the first time in his life. Most likely it would be the last time, too. In another minute, however, he had forgotten about being afraid. He was smiling and excited. His heart was going bump, bump, bump, like a drum beating inside him. It sounded to Peter as if it were saying, "To die will be an awfully big adventure."

The Mermaids, when they had sung all the songs they knew, went back one by one to their bedrooms under the sea. Peter heard the tiny bells on their doors ringing, *ting-ting*, as the Mermaids shut their doors behind them. The waters were now lapping round his feet, and there was nothing to do but wait till they washed him off the rock. He saw a curious thing floating on the lagoon; it looked like a piece of paper. He thought it might be a part of the kite, until he noticed that it was moving against the tide. Indeed, it seemed to be trying to come up to him. And presently it did come, right up to the rock. It was not a piece of paper, it was the Never-Bird, on her nest with eggs in it. She had managed to steer with her wings, but was very tired. She had come to rescue Peter, because (as you have heard) he had been kind to her when her nest fell out of the tree.

She told Peter that she wanted to give him her nest to get ashore in. But it took him such a long time to understand her, that they grew quite cross, and called each other names. Until at last the Never-Bird gave the nest one great shove, and flew up off the eggs. Then Peter saw what she meant, and he was really grateful. He thought it would be a shame to squash the eggs, so he put them into a deep tarpaulin hat, which had been left by the Pirate Starkey during the fight. It was quite water-tight, and he set it afloat. The Never-Bird was ever so pleased. She got into the hat, Peter got into the nest, and they cheered each other like mad. Then they drifted apart from each other. And it was only a little while before Peter reached the house under the ground – nearly as soon as Wendy, who had been some time coming home, because the kite liked carrying her and had not hurried.

Everybody was delighted to see everybody else. And as Peter had to be bandaged, the other boys wanted bandages too. And, what with telling their adventures, and one thing and another, they were several hours late for bed. It was perfectly lovely.

10

The Redskins and the Pirates

The Redskins now became the children's best friends, especially Tiger-Lily, who could not forget how Peter had saved her from the hands of Smee and Starkey. She said: "Peter Pan save me, me his very nice friend. Me no let Pirates hurt him." She and her braves sat all night and every night, keeping guard above the underground house. And the Redskins also took to kneeling at Peter's feet, and called him the Great White Father. This was very pleasant for Peter, and he gave himself fine airs over it. But the Redskins were nothing like so polite to the other boys. They just said, "How do," or something like that. Perhaps they thought Peter had done *all* the fighting in the lagoon by himself; but *we* know how the Boys had helped.

One evening, the Redskins were on guard above, and the children were having tea below. It was a make-believe tea, which is never so interesting as a real one, and there was a good deal of quarrelling going on. They kept telling tales of each other to Wendy; it was all one string of complaints:

"Slightly is coughing on the table."

"Nibs is speaking with his mouth full."

"Curly is trying to eat rolls and yams at once."

"I complain of the Twins." And so on, and so on. It was as well that Peter came in just then with some real nuts for the Boys, and the right Crocodile time for Wendy; she was very particular about the time when it was getting towards bedtime – and the clock inside the Crocodile was the only one on the Island.

The Boys wanted some exercise after their large make-believe tea, and Wendy, as she sat mending a pile of stockings, said they could do a song and dance when their night-gowns were on. So they had a really wonderful dance, with a pillow fight mixed up in it. They tumbled over each other all round the room and pretended to be afraid of their own shadows, and banged each other with the pillows as they sang and shouted. It was the jolliest evening ever known in the house under the ground.

At last, very tired and happy, they got into bed and asked Wendy to tell their favourite story – the story Peter hated – the one about Mrs Darling. This time Peter did not stop his ears, or leave the room, as usual. He stayed where he was, upon his mushroom stool.

Wendy began: "There was once a gentleman—"

"I had rather he had been a lady," said Curly.

"Be quiet," said Wendy. "There was a lady, too."

"She isn't dead, is she?" said the Twins.

"Oh, no."

"I am awfully glad she isn't dead," said Tootles.

"Oh, dear," sighed Wendy, "do let me get on."

"Less noise there!" cried Peter.

"The gentleman's name was Mr Darling," Wendy continued, "and the lady's name was Mrs Darling."

"I knew them," said John proudly.

"I think I knew them," said Michael, but he was not really sure.

"They had three children," said Wendy, "and these children had a nurse called Nana. But Mr Darling was angry with Nana, and he chained her up in the back yard. And so all the children flew away."

"That's an awfully good story," said Nibs.

"They flew away," continued Wendy, "to the Never-Land. But they knew that their mother would always leave the window open for her children to fly back into the nursery. So they stayed away – O, for years – and had a most delightful time. Then they went home and lived happily ever after."

Here there was a deep groan from Peter, which made Wendy afraid he must be ill. She put a kind hand on his waist, and asked him whereabouts the pain was.

"Not that kind of pain," he told her. "It's because you are quite wrong about mothers. They're not like that. They *don't* leave the window open. I know, for I flew away from home and stayed away a long, long time. I made sure I could always get in again. I've never told you before, but when I *did* fly back, the window was barred; my mother had forgotten me, and there was another little boy in my bed."

This may not have been quite true, but Peter believed it. So did all the rest.

John and Michael were so alarmed at the thought of being shut out, that they cried to Wendy: "Let us go home at once!" and clung round her.

"But not tonight!" exclaimed the Lost Boys.

"Yes – tonight, at once," said Wendy firmly.

"Peter, will you please arrange for us to go home?"

"If you wish," replied Peter carelessly, and he went up-tree and ordered the Redskins to take the three children to the coast. Tinker Bell was to guide them over the sea. This really pleased Tink no end, but at first she refused, and Peter had to be very stern with her.

The Lost Boys were so distressed at their mother Wendy going away that they talked of chaining her up and keeping her prisoner. But they took care not to say this in front of Peter. After all, she was Peter's visitor. You can't chain up somebody else's visitor.

Peter, however, did not seem to mind losing Wendy. He did not even say, "Must you go so soon?" or, "Do stay a little longer." He made-believe he didn't care. And he pretended so well, that Wendy fancied he was, on the whole, rather glad to get rid of her, which was very sad, after their beautiful times together.

John and Michael were ready dressed for their journey, when Wendy suddenly thought how nice it would be to invite the Lost Boys to come home with her and be adopted by Mr and Mrs Darling.

When she told this to the Boys, they jumped for joy. "Peter, can we go?" they cried eagerly.

"All right," said Peter. They began to look for sticks and to pack up bundles. But when Wendy told Peter to get *his* things, he skipped about the room, playing on his pipes, and said *he* wasn't coming with her. He meant to stay always a little boy, and have fun in the Never-Land.

"If you find your mothers," he said to the Lost Boys, "I hope you will like them!" They remembered that Peter did not think much of mothers. Wendy hoped, though, to the very last minute, that Peter would change his mind. She put his medicine ready for him, carefully counting the drops – it was only water, but you can't be too particular with medicine; and she made him promise to change his clothes if he got wet. And still she hoped he would say something nice. But he shook hands with her cheerfully, and shouted to Tinker Bell to lead the way. "Now, then, no fuss," he cried to the Boys. "Goodbye, Wendy."

She answered in a choky voice: "Goodbye, Pete— But she never finished his name. For the most fearful, frightful, fierce and furious noise broke out above their heads. The Pirates had attacked the Redskins!

The air was full of deafening screeches, yells, war-cries, bangs of muskets, clashes of steel. And the sound of heavy trampling feet rushing to and fro made the ground shake.

Everybody down below was shaking too – except Peter. Everybody's face was pale, everybody's mouth was open, everybody's feet were stone cold – except Peter's. Peter was feeling as brave as anything. He took his sword in his hand, and his eyes grew very bright and sparkling.

11

The Bravery of Tinker Bell

Hook and his horrible crew had behaved most unfairly to the brave Redskins. Of course, you would expect Hook to be unfair; look at the way he bit Peter! But the Redskins were taken quite by surprise, because for hundreds of years it had always been they who attacked the Pirates first, before daybreak. They never dreamed that the Pirates would attack *them*, in an evening. So they were not ready for a big fight, and most of them were killed, while the rest only just managed to run away. You will be glad to hear that Tiger-Lily escaped.

But the children, down underground, knew nothing of all this. They listened in dead silence to the awful row going on above. And Peter, when things got a bit quieter, told the others: "If the Redskins have won they will beat their tom-tom. They always do if they have had a victory."

Hook was listening down the chimney, and when he heard this he had the tom-tom beaten at once, so as to play a trick on the children. For it was not the Redskins he was really after, but the Boys and Peter Pan. The tom-tom sounded twice; then Hook heard Peter crying, "An Indian victory!" and the children answering, "Hurray!" Hook wondered why they also said, "Goodbye, Peter." But he and his gang were only waiting to pounce upon them. The children came hurrying up the hollow trees – and were seized at once by the sly, deceitful Pirates. They were thrown from one hand to another, till they reached the

Blackamoor. He gagged every one of them, and tied them like a parcel.

Wendy was the last to come out of her tree; and there were all her Boys taken prisoner. Hook bowed, much too politely, and made her take his arm. Soon she, too, was tied and gagged. Then Hook had the nine children chucked all anyhow into the Little House, and it was carried off to the ship by four Pirates, while the rest marched behind, bellowing their hateful song.

Hook returned to hunt for Peter, and he managed to get down the hollowest tree, which was Slightly's. Slightly had got so swelled out with always drinking a lot of water when he was hot (a dangerous thing to do), that he had secretly enlarged his tree to fit him. Otherwise Hook could never have squeezed in.

The Pirate captain peeped through a chink when he came to the bottom of the tree. There was Peter, asleep in the big bed. And he looked so sweet as he lay asleep that Hook felt almost kind towards him – for half a minute. But, unfortunately,

Peter also looked so disgustingly conceited that Hook began to hate him more than ever. If there was one thing that Hook really could not stand, it was somebody else being conceited.

He found he was unable to open the room door. But he had a bottle of deadly poison in his pocket, and he reached his arm through the chink and poured five drops into Peter's medicine. Wendy had put the dose there all ready for Peter to take, but he had left it on purpose, because he thought it would have annoyed her if she knew.

Hook was sure now that he had done for Peter, and he climbed up the tree again, feeling extremely contented.

Peter slept till ten o'clock or so; then he sat up in bed and cried, "Who's that?" for he heard someone tapping at the door. He grasped his dagger and cried again, "Who are you?"

Then a soft, low tinkle answered him: "Let me in, Peter."

Tinker Bell! How could it be, when she had gone over the sea as a guide with the children?

But it was. She was ruddy, and muddy, and excited. In two Crocodile-ticks she had told Peter how Wendy had been captured with the Boys.

Peter cried, "I'll rescue her." But, as he rushed for his sword and dagger, he noticed his medicine. He thought, "I may as well take it before I go. Perhaps I may never come back, and then the medicine will be wasted."

Just as he was putting his hand on the cup, Tink shrieked, "No! Don't!"

"Why not?"

"Hook has poisoned it."

"Nonsense! How could Hook get down here?"

Tink could not explain that; but she said she had heard Hook muttering to himself in the forest, and boasting that he had poisoned Peter.

Peter said: "That's perfect rubbish. Hook could not have been here without my seeing him, and I haven't been to sleep."

Tink could not stop to argue. She got between his lips and the cup, and drank the medicine at one gulp.

Then she turned pale and staggered, while Peter was shouting, "How dare you drink my medicine!"

"It *was* poisoned," Tink whispered faintly. She managed to flutter up to her little room in the wall, and sank upon her couch. Her light grew weaker every moment. Peter knelt by her tiny doorway, and sobbed: "Oh Tink, you did that to save me!" He could see that she was nearly dead. If her light went right out, nothing could save her.

Then he thought he heard her whispering, in a wee thin voice, that she thought she might get well again if children said they believed in fairies.

And he called out to all the children in the world: "If you believe in fairies, clap your hands! Hurry, or Tink will die! Do you believe?"

There was a sound of clapping – it was far away, but certainly it was clapping, quite a lot of clapping. It stopped as suddenly as it began, and behold, Tink was well again! Her light grew bright again, her tinkle came back, and she popped out of bed and went flashing round the room. Peter felt it was quite safe to leave Tink now, while he set out to rescue Wendy.

He had no notion whereabouts to look for her, for Tink was not sure which way the prisoners had been taken. Snow had fallen, so Peter could see no footmarks. He could not hear a sound, or notice anything moving, until the Crocodile passed him, trailing itself slowly and steadily.

Peter decided to follow the Crocodile. He knew it was on the track of Hook.

"It is Hook or me this time!" thought Peter. "One or the other has got to be killed!" And, feeling very cheerful, very happy, and very conceited, he went crawling cautiously after the Crocodile.

12

The Fight on "The Jolly Roger"

The Pirate brig, *The Jolly Roger*, had only one green light showing that dark night, and not a man on guard, for nobody was likely to attack her. The Redskins were defeated, the Boys were captured, the Wild Beasts could not swim, and the Mermaids had other things to think about.

So the Pirates were lying about the deck doing

next to nothing, and Captain Hook was pacing to and fro. He was gloomier than ever. Very likely it was because he had no enemies left to keep him lively (for, of course, he believed he had poisoned Peter). Anyhow, he was feeling very dull.

By and by, to amuse himself, this ill-tempered man had all the eight Boys dragged up from the hold and set in a line before him. The gags and ropes had been removed, but each boy was chained so that he could not fly.

Hook told them, "I am going to make six of you walk the plank tonight" – "drown you," he meant – "but I have room for two cabin boys."

The Boys didn't say "Oh!" but that is what they thought. Just "Oh!"

Hook was impatient. He growled: "Well, which of you will come along with me in the good ship *The Jolly Roger?*"

Tootles stepped forward and replied politely that he didn't think his mother would like him to be a pirate. He winked at Slightly, who said exactly the same. So did Nibs; so did one of the

Twins. Hook was too much vexed to ask the others. He picked out John and Michael – who were, he thought, somehow different from the rest – and they were rather pleased at the idea of being pirates. Hook said they should be called Redhanded Jack and Blackbeard Joe. Indeed, they had nearly settled to join his crew – but they found, before it was too late, that if they did, they would have to cry: "Down with the King!"

Then they both flatly refused.

Hook and his crew were furious. They boxed the boys' ears, and Hook roared: "Get the plank ready. And bring up their mother to see them die."

Wendy saw Hook looking very grim, and her boys looking very pale. She also saw the dirtiest, dingiest, grimiest deck that hadn't ever been cleaned in years.

She thought, "What pigs these Pirates are!"

Hook spoke to her in his horrid polite way: "Now you are about to see your children walk the plank. Silence, everyone! Let us hear a mother's last words to her children."

Wendy glanced at Hook with such scorn that he nearly fainted. She said: "My last words, dear boys, are a message from your real mothers. If they were here they would say, 'We hope our sons will die like English gentlemen.'"

"I am going to do what my mother hopes," cried Tootles.

"So am I," said Nibs.

"So am I," said a Twin.

Before the others could answer, Hook, in a fearful rage, bade Smee tie Wendy to the mast. And the Boys stared at the plank which they had got to walk. The end, where it left off, was over deep water; and that was to be the end of them, too. They felt miserably cold and shaky, and getting less like English gentlemen all the time. Hook was about to order them to move one by one along the plank, but first he thought he would hold Wendy's head fixed, so that she couldn't help seeing them. As he stepped towards her, grinning hatefully—

Tick, tick, tick, tick!

Hook fell in a heap on the deck. If the Crocodile was wriggling aboard, he could not possibly escape. The crew gathered round him to hide him, if they could. They could fight poor harmless children, but they were afraid to tackle the Crocodile.

The eight Boys got away from the plank, and rushed to the ship's side to watch the Crocodile climbing up.

But it wasn't the Crocodile. It was Peter, ticking as loud as he could. He made a sign to them not to cry out, and climbed up to the deck. When he saw the Pirates trying to hide Hook, he was astonished, for Hook seemed quite limp and scared, as if he had heard the Crocodile coming.

Now, as it happened, the Crocodile had lost its tick that night. Its clock had run down, and Peter had been doing the ticking himself, so as to pass safely through the Wild Beasts. The Crocodile was lonely without its tick, so it followed Peter.

A Pirate came up from below; Peter struck deep with his dagger. The Boys threw the body overboard.

"That's one!" said Slightly.

Peter tip-toed into the cabin. The ticking stopped. Smee told Hook that the Crocodile had gone. Hook stood up and began to croak a verse of the Pirate song, to frighten the Boys before he drowned them:

> *"Yo-ho, yo-ho, the frisky plank,*
> *You walks along it so,*
> *Till it goes down and you goes down*
> *To Davy Jones below!"*

Even worse, he took to dancing and pulling faces at the children; and worst of all, he commanded that they should first be flogged with the cat-o'-nine-tails and then walk the plank. He told one of the crew, Jukes, to fetch the cat-o'-nine-tails out of the captain's cabin.

Jukes went for it, and suddenly there was a piercing scream. It was followed by a ringing crow.

"What was that?" said Hook.

"Two," said Slightly.

Cecco the Italian went into the cabin and came out in a hurry. He gasped: "The cabin is as black as a pit, and Bill Jukes is stabbed; and a terrible thing is in there, crowing."

"Fetch it out," said Hook. Cecco was afraid to refuse – Hook's claw was too near him. He crept into the cabin. There was another yell and another crow.

"Three," said Slightly.

"Someone has got to fetch out the doodle-doo," said Hook. "I think it will be Starkey." But Starkey jumped overboard rather than obey orders.

"Four," said Slightly.

Then Hook went in, and Slightly was wanting to say "Five," but Hook appeared again, and said something had blown his lantern out.

And the crew, seeing what a cowardy-custard

their captain was, began to turn against him. Hook was very angry at their jeering, and he thought, as he could not punish the men, he would punish the children. He ordered them all (except Wendy who was still tied to the mast) to be shut up in the dark cabin. He said: "Let them and the doodle-doo kill each other."

Then the captain and the Pirates listened hard. They hoped they would hear eight screeches . . . But the minute the Boys were in the cabin with Peter, he unlocked their chains with a key he had found there, and armed them with Hook's best weapons. They stole out and hid about the deck, while Peter cut the cords round Wendy, sent her to hide, and stood by the mast, where she had been, with her cloak wrapped round him.

Then he gave a most enormous crow.

When the Pirates heard this crow, they thought it meant that the eight Boys had been slaughtered by the doodle-doo thing in the cabin. And they were frightened nearly out of their wits. They began to blame Hook for everything, and to say openly that a man with an iron claw brought bad luck to a ship.

But Hook said: "Oh, no, it all comes from having a girl on board. That always was unlucky for a pirate vessel. Fling her overboard," he cried, pointing to Wendy (as he thought).

The Pirates would have liked to keep Wendy for their mother. But they were so used to doing what Hook told them, that they rushed at the figure by the mast, saying, "No one can save you now, missy!"

"There's one who can," replied the cloaked figure.

"Indeed! Who?"

"Peter Pan!" Down fell the cloak, and Hook, with staring eyes, beheld his worst enemy.

The Pirate captain and his crew understood now who it was that had been stabbing and crowing in the cabin, and they did not see how they had any chance against such a boy as that. However, Hook commanded his men to cut Peter down; Peter called his Boys around him, and a furious fight took place. The Pirates could easily have won if they had kept together. But, what with one thing and another, they had quite lost their heads. They were killed and thrown overboard, quicker than Slightly could count them. Until at last there was no one left alive but Hook.

The Boys were too excited to remember their promise to Peter about not attacking Hook. They were striking at him savagely from all sides, when Peter dropped in among them and cried: "Halt! This man is mine!"

There was never a fiercer battle than what now was seen. Hook had his great sword and his iron claw; Peter had his small sword and his little dagger. It was hard to say which was the quickest and the cleverest. But at last Hook was wounded, and caught sight of his own blood, which, as you know, was a very ugly colour, and always upset him. And the long and short of it is, the wicked Hook saw he was getting the worst of it. And when he had even tried to blow up the powder magazine and failed, then, rather than face Peter's dagger and the sight of his own blood any longer, he cast himself straight into the sea.

The Crocodile, which had silently followed Peter to the ship, had lost its tick, but it found James Hook. This shows that, if you wait long enough, you will get whatever you have waited for. It never does to be too impatient.

13

The Children Home Again

It was perfectly splendid for Peter and the Boys to have a Pirate brig of their own. They dressed themselves in the Pirates' clothes, and Peter, of course, became captain. Strange to say, he tried to imitate Hook, even though he did not look a bit like him. He even smoked Hook's cigars; but not for long.

Wendy was kept very busy altering grown-up suits to fit the Boys, also making plans with John and Michael as to how they should rush home to No. 14 and be welcomed by Mr and Mrs Darling. But Peter kept very dark and silent about *his* plans, and he was so strange and Hookish that nobody liked to ask him questions.

Meanwhile, there has never been time to tell you what was going on at No. 14. Mrs Darling was very unhappy without her children, but she was so sure they would come flying back to her that she stayed at home every day, with the nursery window open, and Nana beside her, waiting and watching.

Mr Darling was unhappy too, of course, but he got more enjoyment out of it, because everybody was talking about him, and he liked that. He was living in Nana's kennel. He said, if he had not been cross with Nana and chained her in the yard, she would have been able to take care of the children. So Nana must be better than he was; and she

could live all over the house, but he should stay in her kennel. He went to his office and back in the kennel every day; he was even asked to parties in it. This helped him to bear the loss of the children.

On a certain Thursday evening – about two days after Peter became captain of the brig – Mr Darling was asleep in the kennel, and Mrs Darling was playing the piano in the day nursery, when two figures darted in at the open window, and immediately shut and fastened it. These were Peter and Tink. Peter wanted Wendy to come home and find herself barred out, so that she would have to go back with him to the Never-Land. This was not nice of Peter; in fact, it was more like a bad imitation of Hook.

But Mrs Darling soon began to cry softly, and Peter knew she wanted Wendy so very much – perhaps as much as he did. He thought, "We can't *both* have her." Then he found he was not so heartless as he had meant to be, and he opened the window again, cried, "Come along, Tink," and was gone. Wendy, John and Michael flew in a minute later. They were puzzled to see Mr Darling asleep in the kennel instead of Nana; and then they heard music in the next room. Mrs Darling had gone on playing.

Wendy peeped in and said: "It's mother."

John peeped in and said: "So it is."

Michael said: "Then, Wendy, aren't you really our mother?"

Wendy did not want to startle Mrs Darling too much, so they each slipped into bed (their beds were always kept ready aired); and when Mrs Darling came in, she thought she was dreaming, until the three children jumped out and hugged her tight.

Then Mr Darling and Nana had to be hugged too. And there was, oh, such a kissing, and cuddling, and purring over each other! After all, the Never-Land was very jolly, but there's no place like home.

Peter saw it all, staring through the window. And he was not so sure as he had been that mothers were silly. This one seemed quite sensible, anyhow.

Mr and Mrs Darling decided to take the Lost Boys for their own, as Wendy had said they would. And they wanted to have Peter, too. But Peter said: "No, Wendy's mother, no one is going to catch me and make me into a man." He explained that he should live with Tink, in Wendy's Little House, which the fairies were going to fix up in the high tree-tops.

Then Wendy wanted so much to go back and see the Little House in its new place, that Mrs Darling had to promise she should go for a week, once a year, to the Never-Land, and spring-clean the Little House – if Peter would come and fetch her.

"You won't forget, will you, Peter?" said Wendy.

Peter said of course he wouldn't, and flew gaily away. But after the first two years (when they had the happiest of times together), Peter did forget. And he came only once more, with one year missed out. He had forgotten Hook; he had forgotten Tink; and now he forgot Wendy. She minded very much, of course, but she knew he was shockingly bad at remembering.

Fifteen years passed. All the Boys were grown up, and could not fly in the least, and the Island had gone right out of their heads. Wendy was married, and had a little girl called Jane; and Jane loved to hear her mother's stories about Peter. She listened till she knew them pretty well by heart. But, one evening, when Wendy had put her child to bed, and was sitting sewing by the nursery fire (just as Mrs Darling used to do), the window blew open, and there was Peter Pan. He had come to fetch Wendy for the spring-cleaning.

She had to tell him that she was a big woman now, and could not fly. At first Peter wouldn't believe this. He was very much distressed; and when he found Jane in the bed, he knew Wendy was not going to mother him any more. He sat crying on the floor. Wendy went out of the room, trying to think of something to comfort him.

Jane woke, saw Peter, and asked him why he cried. He bowed to her politely, and straight away he and she were talking just as he and Wendy had done long ago. They got on so well, and so fast, that, when Wendy came back, what did she find? Why, Jane flying round the room, and Peter seated on the bed-post, crowing like anything! He said Jane was his mother, and she was coming back with him now to the Never-Land. Jane said Peter's spring-cleaning must be done, and Wendy had to let her go, though only for a week. Wendy was dreadfully anxious about it, because goodness knows what may be happening in the Never-Land. But Jane would not be stopped.

As time went by, however, when Wendy was quite old, Jane became a grown-up herself, and had a little girl called Margaret. Jane found she couldn't fly any more, so now she says nothing except, "Take care of her," when Peter comes to fetch Margaret to the Little House in spring. Margaret makes a very sweet mother for Peter. I suppose it will go on like that for ever. The strange thing is, that while none of the Boys remember even the name of the Never-Land, Wendy and her daughter and her granddaughter are still such loving friends with Peter Pan.

About J. M. Barrie, Mabel Lucie Attwell, Peter Pan and Great Ormond Street Hospital

J. M. Barrie was a novelist and a playwright who penned many wonderful works. However, of all of these, his story of Peter Pan, the boy who refuses to grow up, is his most iconic and best-known work. Peter Pan first appeared in Barrie's 1902 adult novel *The Little White Bird*, and he went on to write a play called *Peter Pan, or The Boy Who Wouldn't Grow Up*, which was originally performed in London in 1904. Following the success of the play, Barrie wrote a novelisation of the story which was published in 1911 as *Peter and Wendy*. The novel proved so popular that Barrie approved an abridged version for younger children, written by May Byron. With Mabel Lucie Attwell's original illustrations, this version of Peter's story became one of the iconic Peter Pan editions.

Mabel Lucie Attwell was born in London in

1879. She sold her first drawings at the tender age of sixteen and was a huge commercial success in her lifetime – she produced Christmas cards for the Royal Family, illustrations for magazines, advertising campaigns and artwork for several children's classics, including *Alice in Wonderland*. Her illustrations for *Peter Pan and Wendy*, first published in 1921, were requested by J. M. Barrie himself to accompany May Byron's retold text for younger readers.

In 1929, Barrie gifted Peter Pan and its copyright to Great Ormond Street Hospital for Children in London. This extraordinarily generous bequest meant that his timeless story would directly benefit sick children. As Barrie said in a speech in 1930, "At one time Peter Pan was an invalid in the Hospital for Sick Children, and it was he who put me up to the little thing I did for the hospital." A memorial tablet to Sir James Barrie in the hospital chapel, the Peter Pan Ward, the Tinker Bell play area and the Peter Pan statue at the entrance of the hospital are among the constant reminders to patients and visitors of this amazing legacy. Barrie's name – and Peter's – will always hold a special place in the hearts of patients and their families, as well as everyone who works at the hospital.

Turn the page for

more fun in the Never-Land

Quiz

Now that you've read *Peter Pan and Wendy*, can you answer the following questions about their adventures?

1. What does Peter Pan lose when he first flies through the Darlings' window?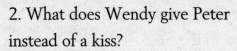
a) Tinker Bell
b) A button
c) His shadow

2. What does Wendy give Peter instead of a kiss?
a) A thimble
b) A shoe
c) John's hat

3. Where do fairies come from?

a) The first time a baby ever laughed, that laugh broke into a thousand pieces and they turned into fairies

b) They are creatures from under the sea

c) They are rays of sunlight that have managed to escape the sun and now live in the Never-Land

4. What creature ate Captain Hook's right hand after Peter Pan cut it off?

a) A crocodile

b) A bear

c) A wolf

5. Where do the Lost Boys live?

a) In a flying house

b) On a boat

c) Under the trees

6. Tinker Bell plays a nasty trick on the Lost Boys when she tells them that Peter Pan wants them to shoot Wendy. Which Lost Boy actually hits Wendy with an arrow?
a) Nibs
b) Slightly
c) Tootles

7. What object saved Wendy when the Lost Boys shot at her?
a) Peter's button
b) A plate
c) Her glasses

8. What creature rescues Peter from the rock on the lagoon?
a) A mermaid
b) A Never-Bird
c) A wolf

9. What is the name of Captain
Hook's right-hand-man?
a) Smee
b) Smelly
c) Salty

10. Tinker Bell sacrifices herself to save
Peter's life. How does she do this?
a) She is shot
b) She is stabbed
c) She drinks poison

11. What do Captain Hook
and his pirates cook to try and
capture the Lost Boys?
a) A green cake
b) Pasta
c) Toast

12. Where had Mr Darling been sleeping whilst the children were in the Never-Land?

a) His bedroom

b) Nana's kennel

c) The kitchen

145

Wordsearch

Can you find all the following words from *Peter Pan and Wendy* hidden in the grid opposite?

PETER PAN	TIGER LILY
WENDY	FAIRIES
CAPTAIN HOOK	MERMAIDS
TINKER BELL	CROCODILE
THE LOST BOYS	PIRATES
NANA	THE NEVER-LAND
THE JOLLY ROGER	

J	F	S	G	B	X	M	A	R	C	G	P	N	Y	T	P
A	C	R	O	C	O	D	I	L	E	T	H	I	E	H	O
F	A	H	P	I	R	A	T	E	S	Q	R	L	S	E	A
I	P	U	K	E	B	A	G	H	E	E	R	A	P	L	T
M	T	Z	S	F	T	I	G	E	R	L	I	L	Y	O	H
G	A	C	H	I	L	E	R	F	A	I	R	I	E	S	E
C	I	M	A	F	O	D	R	Y	J	L	O	T	W	T	N
A	N	D	Y	M	O	R	M	P	W	Z	M	A	W	B	E
F	H	J	H	L	M	E	R	M	A	I	D	S	N	O	V
I	O	M	O	R	Y	B	X	W	E	N	D	Y	L	Y	E
M	O	T	I	N	K	E	R	B	E	L	L	Q	P	S	R
X	K	G	K	A	L	A	N	A	G	E	L	U	O	G	L
W	A	I	K	N	I	J	M	Q	W	O	P	I	G	N	A
M	O	E	N	A	M	J	F	W	Z	P	N	I	A	S	N
T	H	E	J	O	L	L	Y	R	O	G	E	R	E	B	D

Draw Your Own

J. M. Barrie created many wonderful characters in *Peter Pan and Wendy,* and Mabel Lucie Attwell drew her idea of what they might look like. If Peter Pan came and whisked you away to the Never-Land, which character would you be? Maybe you'd be a Lost Boy living in your very own hollow tree, a Pirate on *The Jolly Roger,* a Mermaid swimming in the lagoon, a Fairy flying up in the tree-tops or a Wild Beast (would you tick like the crocodile?)! Can you draw your very own Never-Land character here and overleaf?